To Briony
With love!
from Lucile
Oct. 2006

Daisy the Giraffe

illustrated by
L u c i l e   W a r e i n g
& S a b i n e   V i t t i n g h o f

b y   W i l l   W a r e i n g

Published by Ferdinand Books 🐾

First Edition

ISBN 0-9545491-2-0

A copy of this book is available from the British Library.

Text copyright © Will Wareing 2005
Colour illustrations (full page) copyright © Sabine Vittinghof 2005
Black & White illustrations copyright © Lucile Wareing 2005
Design consultant: Lisa Pampillonia
Narrative consultants: Guy and Edward Wareing

Printed in Hong Kong by Regal Printing Ltd.

to
Lottie

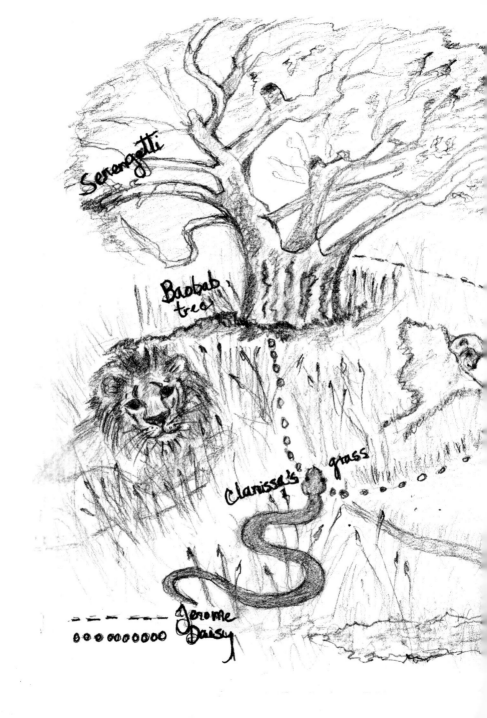

Serengetti

Baobab
tree

Clarissa's grass

- - - - - - Jerome
o o o o o o o o o Daisy

mountains

camp

ite
ound

Village

L W
2004

chapter 1

The Little Boy and the Lion

One hot, sunny day in Tanzania, a little boy was sitting on the ground in the middle of his village, reading a book. Ever since he started the story, he hadn't been able to put the book down – and right now, his eyes were fixed on the page as he mouthed the words quietly to himself.

He didn't notice a lion that was slowly walking towards his back. The lion came right up behind him and poked his head over the little boy's shoulder to see what he was doing. Still, the boy didn't notice he was there, so the lion started reading as well.

After a few minutes, the lion said: "Can't you turn the page, I've already finished this one." Lions are fast readers, you see.

The boy, who was called Jake, turned round to look at him and said loudly: "Will you please be quiet. Can't you see I am busy?"

This kind of thing happened all the time near the Ngorongoro Crater in northwest Tanzania. The crater was an old volcano that had exploded and collapsed in on itself, creating a green, secluded, haven for many animals – and a few people.

Jake's village was just outside the crater and he was very used to lions. He turned impatiently back to the book, muttering that it was always the same, he never got a moment's peace – if it wasn't his little sister Izi pestering him, or a curious animal interrupting him, it would be his parents telling him to hurry up with his chores.

The lion, whose name was Patrick, was a reasonable sort of carnivore and thought he wouldn't bash the boy with his paw for being so rude quite yet. He wanted to know what happened next in the story.

Also it was lonely being in the bush by himself and he wanted some company, even if it was small, impolite and human.

Patrick hung slightly back from Jake, trying not to breathe on him too hard, or tickle him with his whiskers, and he stretched his neck up to look over Jake's shoulder at the pictures in the book.

Patrick could also hear the story because Jake was reading aloud. Patrick liked having stories read to him, especially ones with lions in them.

What Jake was saying was this…

*****

Two lions raised their heads above the long grass and fixed their hard, yellow gazes on a small giraffe, standing alone, away from the rest of the herd.

The giraffe was fat and obviously not very fast. He wasn't paying attention to anything around him and was stuffing wads of acacia leaves into his mouth, humming "yum yum" to himself.

The lions were hungry; they had not eaten in days. One of them had a thick mane but was old and scrawny, with lots of scars on his face from fights through the years. The old lion – Anatole – was also bitter because a pair of younger, stronger lions had driven him away from his pride and he had lost everything.

In order to hunt, he had had to team up with a very young lion, Edvard, who was just starting to learn how to survive for himself in the bush. Edvard was keen and fast, but he didn't listen and was always racing off without a moment's thought. Anatole didn't consider him an ideal hunting partner.

However, he didn't have anyone else to help him and now he was reliant on Edvard.

"Not before my signal," Anatole hissed. Impatient as always, Edvard growled back at him to say he understood.

Together, the lions started to creep forward through the grass. Suddenly, they disturbed a bird, which flew up into the air, crying out loudly.

*****

"Amateurs," snorted Patrick.
Jake turned around and looked at him sternly.
"Sorry," mumbled Patrick.
Jake raised an eyebrow as if to say it was Patrick's last chance and turned over the page...

*****

The lions quickly crouched down, flattening themselves to the ground, and remained absolutely still. Against the long grass of the Tanzanian bush, they were almost invisible.

But the disturbed bird had been noticed by another young giraffe, who was even further away from the adult herd.

This was Daisy. Daisy had the longest eyelashes in the animal kingdom but she wasn't happy. She was too short and the tiny spots on her coat were not flattering at all, or so she thought. She had wandered away from the rest of the herd to feel sorry for herself.

The disturbed bird had startled her and she looked over to where it had come from, holding her head still and her ears forward. But after a minute or so she relaxed, there was nothing there.

But wait, she thought to herself, the grass was moving in a strange way. She looked more closely. A gust of wind parted the grass and she saw the shoulder of a lion tensed and ready to attack.

Her long throat went completely dry, as she followed the line of their bodies towards her only friend in the herd, Bertie. She tried to cry out but no sound would come from her mouth.

The lions had started to move again, stalking forward, preparing to run. Still, she couldn't make a noise. But then she had an idea. She curled her long tongue around the branch of a nearby tree and shook it for all she was worth.

The shaking branches got the attention of the leader of the herd, an enormous giraffe called Jerome. Jerome had so many large dark spots on his coat that he looked almost black. There wasn't an ounce of fat on him, he was 19 feet tall – big even for a giraffe – and he happened to be Bertie's father.

Jerome saw the lions streaking across the grass towards his son and lumbered forward in a desperate run to head them off. For all his awkward style, he was immediately galloping at high speed.

As usual, Edvard had raced ahead. With his eyes fixed on the young giraffe, he was not looking around him. He did not know what hit him as a hoof the size of a dinner plate crashed into his ribs and lifted him bodily off the ground. There was a crunch as

some of his ribs broke and all the wind was knocked out of him.

*****

"Ouch!" yelped Patrick, crinkling up his face.

*****

But Jake did not even pause to look around this time, he was reading how Anatole had stopped running the minute he had caught sight of Jerome. No lions are interested in attacking a fully-grown, adult giraffe – they only have a chance if the animals are young and weak.

Anatole was furious. "Fool," he said quietly, as he saw Edvard slumped painfully on the ground. It was going to take him a long time to recover. He would be unable to hunt for weeks – which meant Anatole was once more on his own. His stomach growled.

He looked over to where Jerome now stood with the young giraffes, with his face twisted in anger and frustration. It was all that young giraffe's fault, he thought – if she hadn't shaken the tree, his belly would be full by now.

But then, his face broke into a smile. If the little one liked being so far away from the other giraffes, then she wouldn't be protected all the time.

Even by himself, he thought he would just about be able to bring down a young giraffe, if she was alone. His features hardened. He might be old, but he was still cunning and he would have that little giraffe.

Meanwhile, Jerome was speaking sternly to Bertie, who still had leaves hanging out of his mouth.

"I don't care if they are the most delicious leaves you have ever eaten, you have got to keep an eye out for danger," insisted Jerome.

"From now on there is to be no wandering off by either of you, unless an adult is with you," he said, "do you understand?"

They both nodded their heads as they looked up at him, towering above them. Jerome then turned away but not before he gave Daisy a wink and said: "Well done for raising the alarm."

Bertie went up to Daisy and offered her the acacia leaves. "I'm so sorry, Daisy," he said, "I find it hard to think about anything when I am eating."

But Daisy wasn't paying any attention. How was she going to get away to consult the ancient baobab tree at the edge of the savannah – where she had heard you could go for the most difficult of problems – when Bertie's father had forbidden them to go anywhere by themselves?

chapter 2

A Snake called Clarisssa

Patrick couldn't keep quiet for a minute longer. He had been looking uncomfortable ever since Edvard had been kicked.

"Those two didn't have a clue," he said. "Everyone knows it is an elementary mistake to sneak up on giraffes – they look sweet and docile but they have the hardest kick in the bush.

"And it is not fair picking on us for trying to eat short fat giraffes, that's what we are here for – natural selection and all that."

Jake fixed him with a beady stare.

"That is just the sort of thing I would expect to hear from you," he said. "Those lions were about to eat Bertie, Daisy's only friend, how could you defend them?"

Jake felt very protective towards giraffes as they were the national animal of Tanzania and everyone loved them.

Patrick looked away and started muttering about the law of the jungle and soft human thinking, but he wasn't quite brave enough to say it out loud.

Meanwhile Jake had turned back to the page...

*****

"Bertie, I need your help," said Daisy. "I must get to the old baobab to ask for advice, because I am not going to stay short and spotty for the rest of my life."

"Daisy, you heard what Dad said," replied Bertie, "I don't even like to think what he'll do if we go away without asking."

"I don't care," said Daisy, "they will never let me go. They will just tell me to exercise patience or something."

"We're going to get into real trouble if we sneak away," said Bertie.

Daisy decided to resort to desperate measures. She looked straight into Bertie's eyes and said: "If you don't come with me, I'll tell your mother about your secret store of wild honey."

"You wouldn't," he cried. Ngorongoro honey tastes better than chocolate and is absolutely irresistible to giraffes.

"I would," she replied, with a steely edge to her voice.

"I'll come with you," said a little voice from the ground. It was a young warthog called Skye who was always following Daisy around.

Daisy peered down. "No way," said Daisy. "You are far too young."

"You never let me play," Skye squealed, and she started making such a racket that Daisy was worried one of the adults would notice.

"Well, all right," she said, "but you have to be quiet and listen." Skye's tail went straight up in the air from delight and she promised she would.

"What about you, Bertie," Daisy asked. "Are you with us?"

Bertie knew it wasn't really a question, there was only one possible answer.

"Okay, okay, I'll come," he said miserably.

Daisy then outlined the plan of escape. They were going to wait till dawn and head off quickly before the rest of the herd realised they were missing.

"I'm sure we will be safe if we all stick together," she said, but mainly to Bertie, who still looked very uneasy.

They managed to get through the rest of the day without looking too suspicious, but all of them were very nervous, and that night no one slept a wink.

Dawn broke and Daisy went to find Bertie, who was trying to

hide behind a bush. Skye materialised between her legs, hopping
around excitedly.

In the half-light, they started walking quickly in the direction
of the sun, where Daisy had heard the baobab could be found. No
giraffe saw them leave but they were followed by one animal.
Anatole the lion was shadowing them, hardly believing that his
chance had come so quickly.

The friends were soon disorientated and did not recognise
their surroundings. They kept on walking for hours and hours.
Daisy was constantly checking the landscape for signs of large
trees, and Bertie was looking grumpier and hungrier by the minute.

Daisy kept them going without a break until they came across
something they had to stop for – a river. She was nervous, rivers
were extremely dangerous. The last thing you wanted to do was step
on a baby hippo and have its furious mother come after you.

On the distant banks she could also see crocodiles, and if
there were some on the bank, there were bound to be others in the

water too. The first part of the river was shallow but it looked fast-moving on the far side.

She came hesitantly down to the water's edge.

"I don't know about this," said Bertie at her side, spreading his legs and taking a drink.

"There is no other way, we have to do it," she said, putting out a tentative hoof into the stream. Daisy had wrapped Skye in her tail and was holding her above the water because it was too deep for the little warthog.

Anatole watched the three of them wading across the river from a high bank. He was concerned. He did not want his revenge ruined by some idle, greedy crocodile. He scanned the far banks for long reptilian tails disappearing into the river.

Daisy, Bertie and Skye had now reached a sand bank in the middle of the river and were having a rest. The water still looked fine, there were no eyes breaking the surface nor suspicious ripples, so they started crossing the deeper stream.

As they hit the centre of the current, an enormous crocodile called Oscar was gliding silently towards them under the water. The corners of his huge mouth, filled with razor-sharp teeth, were curved upwards in an evil grin.

"I luv a nice bit of g'raffe," Oscar grunted to himself, "good n' rotted at the bottom ov river, jerst melts in yer mouf. N' so difficult to get these days."

He knew if he could fix his jaws around one of those dainty legs, he would be lunching on giraffe steak for weeks. He was very bored with fish. "Err fish, I 'ate 'em," he mumbled, "all vose ickle bones stuck in yer teef."

Suddenly Daisy heard noisy splashing behind her, and turned to see a lion racing across towards them. She started to surge out of the water, followed closely by Bertie, and then winced as something tore into her ankle. She caught a glimpse of hundreds of white teeth flicking past her back leg, as she raced up the bank and kept running.

Oscar did not understand why his favourite snack had just leapt away from him, until he glanced back towards the middle of the river and saw Anatole. He opened his jaws wide in defiance and hissed. Anatole held his gaze. Those are my giraffes, his eyes were saying. Eventually Oscar slipped into the river, licking a single drop of blood from his front tooth.

In the meantime, Daisy, Bertie and Skye had kept on running until they couldn't go any further. It was only then that Daisy stopped to look at the cut on her leg. It hurt a bit and was still bleeding but didn't look too serious.

They all decided to stop and rest for a moment. Bertie went to find something to eat. Daisy stopped at the edge of some long grass and standing on her tiptoes, scanned the horizon.

As she squinted to look in the distance, she could feel something brushing against her back leg, but thought it was a bit of grass. But the grass got heavier and she looked down to see a young python racing up her leg, swirling around her back, doing a few loops of her stomach and then tying herself in a neat bow – a flourish typical of young female pythons.

"Jusst ssee if you can get out of thhat," the python said rather smugly.

Daisy was too tired to get upset and she also knew a thing or two about snakes. She looked at this one down the end of her elegant nose, lifted up her tail, which had a bushy tuft on the end, and began to lightly tickle the snake's ribs.

"No, no, you can't do thhhat," the python cried, as she wriggled and squirmed and started to laugh.

"Stooooop," she finally said, as she undid the bow and fell in a heap on the floor.

"That'sss cheating," she lisped. "I have been practisssing that knot for ages and it was my bessst one."

Daisy peered at her through her eyelashes. "Well, you had better practice a bit more," she said. "I didn't think it was very good at all."

Daisy looked at the snake for a little while and then added: "But I will make a deal with you. We are lost and if you help us find the old baobab at the edge of the savannah, I will show you a knot that is secret to giraffes and is famously unbreakable."

The snake was called Clarisssa (snake names normally have lots of 'sss') and her eyes lit up at the thought of a new knot. She said she knew exactly where the old tree was, but it was quite far and they had better start straight away.

Clarisssa slithered on ahead, her tongue darting out to encourage them to follow her. Bertie whispered to Daisy that he had never heard of this famous giraffe knot and Daisy admitted that she hadn't either, but they had better think of one before they got to the tree.

Now they were travelling down paths they hadn't noticed before, little tracks taking them towards the edge of the savannah. When Daisy didn't think she could walk a step further, Clarisssa told them to be quiet because they were approaching the baobab.

Ahead of them was the biggest tree that they had ever seen, with a trunk so wide it would take several minutes to walk around, and a vast canopy of branches.

The rest of them hung back as Daisy went forward cautiously, step-by-step. She didn't know how you were supposed to address trees so she came close to the bulbous trunk of the baobab and whispered into a crack in the bark: "I am the shortest giraffe in the herd and nobody likes me." She paused and added: "Also I don't like my spots. Is there anything I can do?"

She took a step back and waited. Very slowly, almost without her noticing, a branch dropped down around her shoulders. It felt very comforting having the solid wood close to her, and then all of a sudden, she heard a voice vibrating within her.

It was a low, ancient sound and she knew she could trust it.

"Daisy, Daisy, Daisy," she heard the voice resonating in her chest, "time changes everything. Short may become tall and foul become fair, without one even realizing it."

Daisy was a bit frustrated at this advice, but she came forward to whisper respectfully into the bark once again.

"Thank you, but can't I chew a root or something?" she asked, before moving back to snuggle into the branch.

There was a long silence. "Everything comes to those who wait," said the voice eventually, in the tone of one who has been giving the same advice for a very long time. And with these words, the branch withdrew into the canopy.

Daisy was crestfallen. After all her effort to get to the baobab, what it had said was as annoying as her mother or any grown-up. "There must be a way," she said to herself, "I will find it."

At that moment, Clarisssa tried to curl around her ankles and find out how to do the inescapable giraffe knot. Daisy gave her a little boot in the stomach and said: "If I have to wait for an answer, you do too!" And with that, she stalked off to be by herself.

Clarissa was mystified, but knew there was no talking to giraffes who were sulking. So she climbed up the baobab and lay out to sleep on one of its broad branches.

As they slept, Anatole was watching from a nearby boulder. He had taken some time to cross the river, looking for a shallow fjord, so that he wouldn't be attacked by crocodiles. Then he had cut back along the far bank of the river until he found the giraffes' tracks. He followed them easily, especially with drops of Daisy's blood marking the way.

When he saw how isolated the baobab tree was, he thought his moment had come. But despite his hunger and his impatience, he could not approach the giraffes – the baobab was protecting them. Anatole could feel a presence that he could not pass. Any animal accepted under the branches was guarded by the tree. The friends were safe for the night.

chapter 3

Flaming Warthogs

Jake broke off reading and started chewing a fingernail. Patrick tilted his head to look at him.

"All lions aren't like Anatole you know," said Patrick. "He must be a rogue from the Serengeti – they're a rough lot over there, I don't like them."

Patrick himself came from Lake Manyara where the lions had taught themselves to climb trees. They liked to lie on the branches and hang out.

"I'm not like that," he added.

Jake was paying no attention. He had started reading again.

*****

Shortly after dawn that same day, Jerome had discovered that Daisy and Bertie weren't there. He raced out in the direction he thought they might have gone.

Skye's father, Bruce, was also beside himself with worry. He had done a morning roll call of his eleven children, who normally followed him everywhere in a neat little line, and discovered that Skye, his eldest, most adventurous daughter was missing.

Bruce insisted that they go search for them together because although his legs were a fraction of the length of Jerome's, he thought he could keep up. The two of them set off and covered a lot of ground but there was no sign of their children.

The problem was that while Jerome, as the tallest giraffe in the herd, towered above everyone else, Daisy and Bertie were small and not easy to spot in high grass. There was no way anyone was going to spot tiny Skye.

By the middle of the afternoon, Jerome realised that they needed help. They kept on walking and soon came across a baboon, sitting on a termite mound, picking his nose.

Jerome stopped and asked the baboon: "Have you seen two small giraffes and a little warthog passing by here."

"You're 'aving a giraffe," the baboon laughed, clutching his ribs and almost falling off his perch. "Giraffe" was baboon-speak for "laugh". It was widely known in the jungle that baboons liked to rhyme words, but Jerome was not in the mood to play word games with monkeys.

Bruce poked one of his tusks into the baboon's tail and Jerome pulled his neck back as though preparing to thwack the baboon from his seat like a golf ball, and the monkey tried to make amends fast.

"Only jokin'," he said, "nope, I ain't seen nuffink. But if I 'ad, you would be the first to know. Cross my 'eart."

Jerome told him that had better be the case and he walked off followed by Bruce, as the baboon said quietly under his breath that he hadn't seen two giraffes and a warthog, but he had seen two giraffes, a warthog and a snake, heading in the other direction.

"If only people knew the right questions to ask," he mused.

Canice, as that was the baboon's name, thought it might be amusing to watch these two and scampered up the nearest acacia tree to see what happened – because the other thing he had not mentioned, was that there were some humans with guns nearby.

Annoyed by the baboon and out of his normal surroundings,

Jerome wasn't paying as much attention to danger as normal. He walked straight into a trap.

The hunters had camouflaged their vehicles and were concealed downwind, behind some trees. There was a rifle trained on Jerome as he walked into a clearing.

Suddenly Jerome felt a jab in his neck and looked down to see a feathered twig sticking out of himself. He didn't know what it was but it was making him feel very strange, so he turned to run.

As he swung around, his legs felt weak and instead of moving forward, he tripped on a hoof and toppled softly to the ground.

A team of hunters then raced out from behind trees. Their leader was an ex-army officer called Jeremy and he knew he had to work fast. It was difficult working with tranquilizers on giraffes because the pressure of the blood racing up their necks made it risky for them to be on their sides for long.

He wanted this animal alive, to be transported to a nearby park where the giraffe population was being restocked. Jeremy estimated that they had a couple of minutes at best to secure him.

Jeremy was a natural leader and his team was well trained to follow instructions. They quickly had four ropes around Jerome's neck. Two men held onto each rope as Jerome started to come round and get on his feet. But they underestimated his strength. Rearing up on his hind legs, he swung two men clear off their feet, and dragged two others onto their knees.

Still, the ropes held firm and after struggling for a while, Jerome began to tire. Slowly they were able to manoeuvre him towards a truck that had a ramp leading down the back. Jerome was led up the metal ramp, which banged shut behind him, with the sound of bolts on either side being pushed home.

For the first time ever, Jerome felt trapped, closed in. He kicked out with a back hoof into the ramp, which dented the metal with a great hollow ring.

Jerome held his head down in despair and, as he did so, glimpsed Bruce hiding under some nearby bushes. Bruce waited till the men wandered away and crept up to the lorry. Jerome was able to lean over the edge and talk to him. He told Bruce to find help quickly, wherever he could.

"You can rely on me," said Bruce, as he trotted smartly out of the clearing, without any idea of what to do. He carried on running, hardly knowing which direction to go in.

"Looks like you two 'ave run into a spot of bovver," sneered Canice, as Bruce ran by.

"I bet you knew about the men there," fumed Bruce. "Thanks a lot for warning us."

"You never asked," replied Canice. "But I might be able to 'elp… if there was somefin' in it for me."

"That's it, big nose," Bruce shouted as he lost his temper and charged at him, "I'm going to teach you a lesson."

"If that's yer attitude, you can get yer mate out of this mess by yourself," replied Canice, jumping nimbly out of the way.

Bruce slumped, knowing that he could never do it alone.

"All right, all right, but I have nothing to give you," he said miserably.

"In that case," said Canice, "I want you to 'pologise for bein' so rude and then say: 'I am a silly piggy and I need the greatest, cleverest, 'andsomest monkey of all time to 'elp me'."

Bruce's tail went straight and he went bright red in the face from fury but he managed to get the words out.

"Mmm, not bad," said Canice, "but I fink you could do better. Try and say it… wiv' more feelin'."

Bruce lost his composure completely and tried to dig up the tree Canice was in.

"Only teasin', only teasin'," admitted the baboon, "I was always going to 'elp you. Let's go get that leaf-eater out of the box."

The two of them crept back towards the camp. Canice was sure he could undo the bolts on the lorry but they would have to deal with the guard as well.

"Ok piggy, I can get your friend out of that fing, but I need you to 'elp," said Canice, "now listen up 'cos this is the plan…"

*****

Jeremy's workers had gathered around the campfire, discussing their pay. Jeremy wasn't bad to work for, they said, but he was so mean with money. He charged them for cooking fuel and rented their sleeping cots to them. They were talking about the bonuses they could hope for, when a warthog came out of nowhere and jumped through the fire. They couldn't believe their eyes, but it happened again.

Bruce was almost alight by now but he took a few more running leaps through the fire. He had rolled himself in a thick layer of mud to protect himself

31

but he could feel bits of his hair burning.

This was the most terrifying thing he had ever done but it worked. The men called out to their friend who was keeping an eye on Jerome to come and see the flaming hog. The guard walked away from the trailer to join them around the fire.

It was the moment Canice had been waiting for and he leapt lightly onto the back of the lorry, whispering to Jerome to be quiet for he was there to help.

Canice pulled on the first bolt and it easily slid out of its bracket – but the bolt on the other side, which Jerome had kicked, was proving more difficult to budge.

Canice knew he hadn't got long before Bruce's protective mud coat became too hot and he would have to rush to the water pool, but the bolt wasn't moving. Canice threw his shoulder against the door trying to create some room and it slipped a fraction, but it wasn't happening fast enough.

He noticed that the men's interest was wandering as he saw Bruce streaking away out of the corner of his eye. Canice urgently whispered to Jerome that he couldn't do it, the bolt wouldn't move.

"Get out of the way," Jerome said. And lifting his back legs off the ground he hit the door with both hooves. It held firm. All the men around the fire leapt up.

"You can do it," urged Canice, and Jerome hit the door with everything he had got, sending the remaining bracket flying from the side of the truck.

Jerome turned and raced out the back of the truck. Canice managed to get a hand in his mane and pulled himself up onto Jerome's back as they made their escape.

Jeremy was not sure how he had been robbed by a flaming bush-pig and a monkey but he was going to have to make up a good story to cover this one up. At least he could cut the guards' wages, he said to himself.

chapter 4

Educating Daisy

Jerome ran for a long time with Canice on his back, until he was sure the hunters were not following them.

"Thank you for your help," said Jerome, once he had stopped, "Is there anything I can do to repay you?"

"Nah, I fink we're quits," said Canice, "I always wanted to ride a giraffe. If you could give me a turn round the bush from time to time, that should settle it.

"Also, I fink I know where your kids 'ave gone. Most of the runaways 'ead for the baobab close to where the savannah ends. I'll show you the way if you like."

Jerome said he would be grateful and they waited until Bruce caught up with them before setting off.

Canice passed the time by teasing Bruce about his tail, which was slightly singed and smoking. From time to time, he also climbed up Jerome's neck to check his bearings – and only got thrown off once for tickling the bald patch between Jerome's horns.

Before long, Jerome could see the branches of an enormous baobab tree. Soon, he could also make out two little shapes that looked like small giraffes beneath its branches. He broke into a run.

As he got close, a small form bolted out from under the tree and wrapped itself around his legs. Bertie was snuffling quite loudly from the relief of not having to cross the bush without his father again.

Jerome bent down and nuzzled his son's neck.

"What have you been up to, my boy," he said, catching sight of Daisy sheepishly coming forward as well. "I think I can guess whose idea this was."

"Over here, young lady," he called. Daisy approached Jerome with her head lowered.

"It was all my fault," she said, "I forced Bertie to come with me."

"Nobody can force anybody else to do anything," replied Jerome, "but let's not talk about it now, I want to get you all home."

Bruce had to go slightly further to find Skye. She was happily playing in a mud hole. He dived in too as his tail was still a bit sore and they quickly made up. Skye promised she wouldn't go away without telling him again.

After Jerome had gone through the ritual of being wrapped up in a knot by Clarisssa, who was still waiting to learn the unbreakable giraffe knot, they started to head back home. There was no way Canice and Clarisssa were going to be left behind having been through so much together, so they came too.

On the way home, Jerome started forming some pretty rigid ideas about the influence of Daisy on his son. He himself felt

fatherly towards her, as her father had hurt his leg and been dragged down by lions just after Daisy was born.

*****

Jake shot a furious glance at Patrick, who quickly pretended to see something in the other direction.

*****

Daisy's mother had always had trouble looking after her, because even as a young giraffe, Daisy was so head-strong. What she really needed was someone to keep an eye on her. Jerome had another idea and glanced in Canice's direction.

"That might just work," he said to himself.

Later that day, when they were back at home, Jerome started to discuss his plans with his mate, Kate.

"We have to do something," he said, "Bertie is fat and is being led astray by Daisy."

"He just has big bones," she replied, "and, after all, a giraffe's got to eat."

"They don't have to eat that much," he replied. "The boy never stops stuffing himself. I've decided Bertie is going to go to his uncle Tristram's for a year or so. Tristram will lick him into shape – make a real giraffe out of him – and his cousins will be a good influence on the boy."

"I'll take him myself, tomorrow morning first thing," Jerome added.

*****

Daisy had been in agony ever since they got back, wondering

what her punishment was going to be. Her mind kept playing over all the awful things that could happen to her.

When Bertie came to find her the next day, she was exhausted and grumpy but she smiled when she saw him. At least she still had Bertie, she thought to herself. But Bertie was behaving very strangely, he wasn't even chewing on any leaves.

"Daisy, they're sending me away," he said.

"Nooo, you can't go," she cried, "but how long for, it'll only be for a week won't it?"

"A year," he replied. Daisy was too shocked to say anything.

"You can have my secret honey store," he said, "I don't think I am going to need it where I am going."

"I don't want your stupid honey," she sobbed, turning her back on him as she cried.

"I can't believe you are leaving me... and I never want to see you again."

Bertie wanted to give her neck a nudge and find her some yummy leaves like he normally did, but he heard a snort from behind him. It was Jerome calling him away.

A tear welled in his eye too as he walked slowly away with Jerome by his side, who was not taking any chances on the two of them hatching any more escape plots.

"Don't worry, Bertie, she'll be fine, and you'll make lots of new friends at your uncle's," he said.

Meanwhile, Daisy was still crying, and feeling awful for having been mean to Bertie.

"Short, spotty, friendless, can my life get any worse?" she asked herself.

Little did she know that Jerome had some ideas on that front as well.

*****

For the next few weeks, Daisy wandered around looking miserable, refusing to eat anything. Eventually Jerome marched over to her.

"Daisy, I have had enough of you mooching around looking sad and getting thinner," he said. "I have given Canice full authority over you from now on. He is going to report to me whether you are eating your greens.

"Maybe you can learn something from him as well, baboons have a lot of knowledge about the bush," he added. "So make sure you listen to what he has to say."

Canice appeared from behind a tree. "Who is the luckiest giraffe in the 'ole bush?" he cried. "It's you, Daise! The very first pupil of Professor Can!"

Daisy's heart sank.

"So, shorty, what do you want to learn today? We could do termite structures and modern grass patterns. Or even baboon culture, one of my favourites."

Daisy wasn't sure how much of this she could take.

"Whatever," was all she could manage.

"Or maybe we should do units of length first, yes that's it. Let's measure you, because you know what, I fink you might 'ave grown these past weeks."

Daisy's ears pricked up and she reluctantly came over to the tree that Canice was now sitting in.

"Do you really think so?" she asked.

"We'll see soon enuf. Now stand up against the trunk, and stay still. Mmm, a quarter of my tail equals 'alf a section of vine, and that divided by the length of my nose is… minus 40 soldier ants in length. Oh well, bad luck, I fink you've shrunk."

Canice burst out laughing but Daisy gave him a look and he stopped, swallowing hard.

"OK, maybe you 'ave grown a little bit – but no more than

the length of my foot. Anyway, now I've marked the 'eight of your 'ead on this trunk, minus your 'orns which don't count, I'll measure you every month and we'll see how fings go."

"Measssure me too, measssure me too," came a voice from below. It was Clarisssa, who was still hanging around hoping to learn new knots.

Canice wasn't sure whether his job included amusing snakes but a mischievous thought occurred to him.

"OK," he said, "but I'll have to measure you in pieces because you're very long." He measured out one tail's length.

"One... now put your nose on my finger to mark the spot." As she did so, he started to scratch her ribs.

"Ooooh, that tickless," she cried out, twisting and turning, making big loops with her body.

Canice thought she was going to do this and he kept on tickling her and started to thread her tail through every loop her body made, so that soon she was a bundle of knots. Suddenly, she stopped wriggling and said: "Hey, I can't move."

"Can I introduce you to the famously unbreakable baboon knot, better in so many ways than the famously unbreakable giraffe knot."

"Not bad," admitted Clarisssa. "Now let me out."

"That's the fing about famously unbreakable knots, they are... famously unbreakable," he replied. "I couldn't undo you even if I wanted to."

"But I'm sure you'll undo yourself, slippery one... eventually."

"Now Daise, I believe we was talking 'bout famous baboon sayings, let's go find a quieter spot to continue the lesson..."

And with that they left Clarisssa trying to pull her head through the first double twist of her tail.

*****

Anatole didn't think he could stand any more baboon witticisms. He was a stealthy hunter and could normally get close enough to hear what was being discussed, but he never got any opportunities to attack. All he could do was listen and it was driving him mad.

Canice's thoughts on the latest wave of zebra dancers – the grace of Saskia, the twirls of Talitha – might have been interesting to some, but not to Anatole, who only dreamed of sinking his teeth into Daisy's neck.

"Will that baboon and that snake ever leave the giraffe alone?" he asked himself. Anatole was beginning to despair, forced to scavenge anything he could find from the carcasses that the vultures and hyenas discarded.

And his teeth always hurt because the bad meat he was eating got stuck in his gums and rotted there. He soon gave up even trying to pick the rotten scraps of meat from his teeth, as he became obsessed with hunting Daisy.

He was waiting, he knew his chance would come.

*****

Meanwhile, Bertie was going through other torments. For months, Tristram had had him on half-rations – with no wild honey nor any other treats – running endlessly up and down dry sand riverbeds. He was accompanied by his cousins Jimmy and Sam, who had also been sent to Tristram's to be toughened up.

However, all the three of them could think about as they puffed up and down the riverbeds was how long this torture was going to go on for. In the few moments when they weren't exercising, Tristram gave them lectures on their attitude towards trees.

"A tree is not just a meal ticket," he would say, "they are tall, noble, living things, much like us. We must respect them because we depend on them."

"But Uncle Tris," said Jimmy, "we're giraffes not monkeys!"

"I would be proud to be called a monkey, swinging from branch to branch," Tristram said dreamily, "because they live in harmony with the trees... and when have you ever seen a fat monkey.

"You have to remember that all animals and plants co-exist together in the bush, and we have to get on with each other," he said, "apart, of course, from lions, who have an absurd superiority complex.

"They are so proud, they can't see beyond the end of their noses. If only they knew that all the other animals laugh at them for their silly fluffy manes, they would slink away in shame and never show their bushy faces again.

"Now boys, enough talking, first one round that tree and back to me gets an extra leaf for supper."

*****

"Hey," said Patrick, "do you think that's true, they don't really laugh at lions, do they?"

But Jake had already swung around to look at Patrick's mane, and tears of laughter were running down his cheeks.

"It's true, you look like you spend all day at the hairdresser, maybe you'd like my mother to put some plaits in for you." And he howled with laughter.

Patrick didn't know how to react. No one had laughed at him before. He put up a paw and tried to flatten his mane a bit.

*****

Bertie and the other young giraffes learnt quickly, despite being confused about exactly what kind of animals they were supposed to be. They were taught how to harvest the leaves carefully, to take the mature leaves from the branch and leave the young buds to grow.

And little by little they started to enjoy exercising as well, delighting in racing each other up any sandy track they could find.

Daisy was also absorbing everything she could from Canice. She wanted to know what he knew about the plants, flowers and berries around them – especially which ones could make her grow, or lighten the dark splotches that she still hated on her skin.

But in amongst all the questions about growing formulas and skin rubs, Canice managed to teach her which plants to use if she wasn't feeling well, what to do if she had hurt the muscles in a leg, or even if she was wounded by a lion or a poisonous snake.

She particularly liked learning about flowers, and the different properties they had. Often she would just look at their petals, lost in thought, or have a flower tucked behind her ear. If Canice saw her like this, he knew she was thinking about Bertie and for once, would keep his mouth shut.

Daisy sometimes heard news of Bertie from migrating wildebeest, but it was never enough. She counted the months as they went by and never stopped missing him.

chapter 5

Itchy Elephants

It was when the evening sun made everything look golden –
the best time of day, or so Daisy thought – that she first caught sight
of Bertie again.

She was standing at the edge of the clearing, chewing a root
that would help soothe a pulled muscle for Jerome, when a tall
giraffe appeared a short distance away.

She hardly recognised him to begin with. But it was Bertie
for sure. Suddenly she felt very shy. She turned her head, quickly
swallowed the root and pretended not to see him.

He approached her hesitantly and said: "Daisy, is it you?"

She turned slowly and opened and shut her eyes a few times.
She wasn't consciously batting her eyelashes, it was just happening.

"Of course, it's me, Bertie," she fluttered. "Don't you recognise me."

"Of course I do," he said, "it's just that you have, well…
changed."

Bertie looked at the giraffe in front of him, with his lower jaw
ever so slightly open. She was tall, with an impossibly elegant neck,
and the biggest brown eyes he had ever seen. He began to feel a bit
dizzy.

"You have changed too, you know," she laughed. Bertie was
almost as tall as Jerome now, and there wasn't anything plump
about him anymore – apart from his cheeks, which were still rather
round and very Bertie.

"I kept your honey store for you," she said.

"Leaves give me all the energy I need these days," he
replied, but added quickly, "thanks so much anyway."

"I like your flower," he said.

"Oh, it's nothing, they just seem to find their way up there," she said, glancing up towards her left ear.

"Look, I have to go talk to Dad about Uncle Tristram's plan to expand the tree programme," he said. "But I'll come straight back, I want to hear all about what you've done this year."

"OK," said Daisy, "I'd like that."

Bertie did indeed come back as soon as he could and the two of them spent the days and weeks that followed discussing everything that had happened to them.

Bertie taught Daisy how to select the best leaves from the trees and leave the new shoots to grow. He taught her about caring for trees and how to encourage the other animals to do the same.

Daisy half-listened, she was more interested in standing close to him when they were eating leaves or quietly watching him when they were walking along together.

She realised just how much she had missed him. From time to time, she told him a few things about termite social customs, but mainly she just liked being with him.

Sometimes he would let her put a flower behind his ear. But Bertie could not really be distracted much from trees, which were his driving passion now. One afternoon, as they were strolling through the bush together, he saw a little elephant pushing backwards against a tree.

"Look, Daisy, that's exactly the kind of destruction I am talking about, I've got to stop that elephant," he said.

"Can't you leave it, Bertie," she answered. "It's impossible getting elephants to listen to you when they are on the rampage."

But Bertie had already set off.

"Have you really thought about what you are doing, little elephant?" he asked.

"The name's Alice and you can get lost, big giraffe," she

said, pushing with all her might. "I am going to push over this tree, then stomp on it. Perhaps I'll munch on a branch or two, perhaps not."

"Why do you have to push the whole tree over to take a single branch?" said Bertie.

"Because I have a very itchy bottom. And that's what elephants do," she said.

"But you don't have to. If you push over all the trees, then there won't be any left," he argued. "And all the other animals won't have anything to eat or anywhere to shelter from the sun."

"Don't be silly, there are plenty of trees for everyone, just look around you," she said. "Now will you stop bothering me while I smash this one up."

She then hit the tree with a thump from her rump. It didn't seem to do much but the leaves shook violently and what looked like a branch fell down on Bertie.

However, it was not a branch. It was a large green

49

mamba, which had been sleeping and was now very awake and very angry. It reared up in fury and sunk its fangs into Bertie's neck, before slithering away.

Green mambas are highly poisonous, aggressive snakes although not as lethal as their cousins black mambas, the most poisonous land snakes of all.

Bertie immediately staggered back against the tree, already feeling the effects of the poison. Daisy raced to his side.

"It was a green mamba, Daisy," he managed to say.

"Bertie, listen to me very carefully," she said. "I know Canice can heal you but it is going to take some time. Stay calm and try not to move. I will be back as soon as I can."

"Please don't leave me," he said.

"This elephant will look after you while I am away, but I must go," she insisted. With that she raced off to find Canice.

In the meantime, Alice, who was really feeling very sorry now, had wrapped her trunk around Bertie to keep him warm, and was wishing with all her huge heart that he would be all right.

Daisy quickly found Canice and explained to him what had happened.

"Do you remember the pale blue flower we saw on the slopes of the crater yesterday?" he said. "It is the only thing that can save 'im."

"I know some moss that will slow the effect of the poison, but you must run like the wind to find the flower, we 'aven't got much time."

Daisy said she remembered the spot and they both set off at high speed in opposite directions. Daisy's face was a mask of determination, she crashed through bushes, swerving past termite mounds, nothing was going to get in her way.

She found the spot where they had seen the flower but it wasn't there. She searched more closely, beginning to panic, and she caught a glimpse of blue. The flower had been trodden hard into the ground by what looked like the hoof of a gnu.

It would have to do, she said to herself, and ever so carefully collected up the fragments of the flower, which she held between her lips as she began the journey back to where Bertie was.

Anatole was waiting for her in the narrow bend of a dry river. She vaguely recognised the scrawny animal in front of her as she screeched to a halt.

"Let me through," she panted, "no time to waste, I've got to get back to Bertie."

"Oh, I don't think so," said Anatole. "I have had enough of chasing you around listening to that absurd monkey's prattlings. It's now time for a real lesson in the bush.

"By now, your friend will be dead, whatever that baboon thinks he is able to do, but I wouldn't worry," he said, "you are about to join him."

With that, Anatole moved forward menacingly. Daisy turned and he leapt towards her, with his claws out to rake her side. But Daisy was not the same giraffe she had been a year ago. She was a lot bigger, a lot braver, and she was not turning to run – far from it. She moved her weight onto her front legs and kicked backwards with all her might.

As he leapt upwards, one of her back hooves connected directly with his chin, smashing his jaws together so hard that all his rotten teeth sprayed out, and he was knocked clean unconscious.

Edvard, fully recovered now, was watching from a rock. He had been doing rather well by himself, and he couldn't believe Anatole had made the basic mistake of taking on a giraffe the size of Daisy. He doubted the old lion was going to be much of a threat to anyone anymore.

Daisy, however, had hardly paused to look at Anatole as she

jumped over his slumped form and raced to where she had left Bertie. He was a lot worse when she got back to him. He had lost all of his colour and had slumped to the ground.

"You took yer time," said Canice. "Where's the flower?"

Daisy showed him the mangled pieces and his expression darkened.

"I don't know if it's enuf," he said, "but we'll try. Now, chew on the petals together with this moss and put it all into 'is mouth."

She did as Canice said and managed to get most of the mixture into Bertie's mouth. Nothing seemed to happen.

"Please don't die," she begged, "I love you so much. You can't leave me again."

And slowly, ever so slowly, she could see his eyes trying to open and some colour returning to his face.

"Hello, Daisy," he just about managed to whisper, as he saw huge eyes filled with tears swimming in front of him.

After a minute, he even gave her a weak smile.

"You are the luckiest g'raffe alive," Canice said to Bertie. "If Daisy 'adn't been here to find that flower, we wouldn't 'ave been able to 'elp you."

"Now, stay away from snakes, apart from Clarisssa of course, and you should be better soon."

It took some time for Bertie to recover. While he was getting better, Daisy did not leave his side. She found him the best leaves, not worrying if she snapped a branch or two to get to them.

Bertie didn't seem to mind either. He realised he didn't have to go ape about tree conditions, all the animals would find their own way of existing in the bush without his supervision. Alice also came by to visit from time to time, walking carefully around any trees in her way.

From that moment on, the two giraffes were inseparable. Daisy would wrap her neck around Bertie's, just happy that he was there. He would rub his cheek gently against her horns. Over time, they got even closer to each other.

And both of them swore they would never leave each other again, whatever anybody said.

*****

Patrick sat back on his haunches, with tears running down his face.

"That was so moving," he said, snuffling to himself. "If Bertie had died... I mean, it would have been too much."

"You're crying. You are the softest lion I have ever met," said Jake. "At the beginning of the story, you would have been happy to eat Bertie."

"That's not true, I always liked Bertie. And I am not crying, my eyes are watering," said Patrick. "Lions have feelings too, you know," he muttered under his breath.

But Jake was miles away wondering to himself why he didn't have adventures like Daisy and Bertie.

He looked out into the distance, not really seeing anything until two indistinct forms began to take shape before him. He blinked and rubbed his eyes but still they were there, two giraffes walking towards him.

Daisy and Bertie walked into the clearing.

"I like stories as well," Daisy said.

"Me too," said Bertie.

"Just don't tell Canice and Clarisssa that we are here," they said together, laughing. "It's good to have a little peace from time to time."

Jake was shocked; Patrick's jaw was hanging open.

"What kind of stories do you like," Jake said eventually. "I have loads."

"Oh, anything with animals," said Daisy.

"That'll be easy," said Jake, running off to his room to get some books.

Out of the corner of his ear, he thought he could hear a baboon voice saying: "So that's where you are. You know the kind of trouble you get into if me an' Clarisssa ain't round to look after you."

Jake smiled to himself... and chose a new story.

also by the same author:

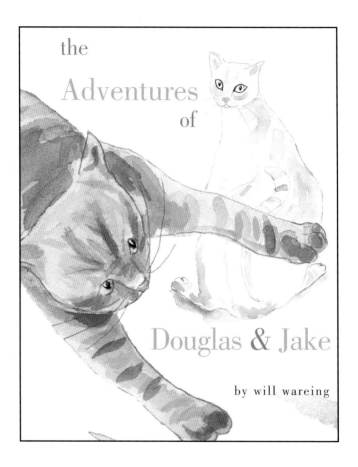

the

Adventures

of

Douglas & Jake

by will wareing